Postcards from • Postales desde

# NEW YORK CITY

Traveling with Anna • De viaje con Ana

⭐ Laura Crawford ⭐

To the people who believed in me, even when I didn't—
Paul Vandersande, Pam Anzalotti, Heidi Roemer and Lisa Steenson

Text Copyright © 2008 Laura Crawford
Illustration and Translation Copyright © 2008 Raven Tree Press

All rights reserved. For information about permission to reproduce selections from
this book, write to: Permissions, Raven Tree Press, a Division of Delta Publishing Company,
1400 Miller Parkway, McHenry, IL, 60050. www.raventreepress.com

Crawford, Laura.
Illustrations by Bonnie Adamson
Book Design by Amanda Chavez

Postcards from New York City / written by Laura Crawford ; translated by Eida de la
Vega = Postales de Nueva York / escrito por Laura Crawford ; traducción al
español de Eida de la Vega — 1st ed. — McHenry, IL : Raven Tree Press, 2008.

p. ; cm.

Text in English and Spanish.

Summary: Join Anna in her travel adventures to the largest
city in the United States, New York City. Child writes postcards
home to friends with facts about historical and tourist sites.

ISBN: 978–0–9795477–2–0 Hardcover
ISBN: 978–0–9795477–3–7 Paperback

1. People & Places/United States — Juvenile fiction. 2. Biographical/United States —
Juvenile fiction.  3. People & Places/United States — Juvenile non fiction.
4. Bilingual books — English and Spanish. 5. [Spanish language materials—books.]
I. Title  II. Title: Postales de Nueva York.

Library of Congress Control Number:  2007939530

Printed in Taiwan
10 9 8 7 6 5 4 3 2 1
First Edition

Raven Tree Press
A Division of Delta Publishing Company
www.raventreepress.com

Hi! My name is Anna. I'm going to New York City with my parents. It is called The City That Never Sleeps and is the busiest city in the United States. Mom said it is unique because it's made up of five sections called boroughs. They are the Bronx, Queens, Manhattan, Staten Island and Brooklyn. I'm glad I saved my money to buy postcards for my family and friends.

¡Hola! Me llamo Anna. Voy a Nueva York con mis padres. La llaman "La ciudad que nunca duerme" y es la ciudad más movida del planeta. Mamá dice que es única porque está formada por cinco secciones llamadas distritos. Ellos son Bronx, Queens, Manhattan, Staten Island y Brooklyn. Me alegra haber ahorrado dinero para poder comprar postales para mi familia y amigos.

Abuelo y abuela,

Wow! New York City is exciting, but I've never seen so many people in a hurry! We went to Grand Central Station to ride the subway. It was too crowded, so we took a taxi. What a mistake! New York is famous for traffic jams. Thousands travel by bus, boat and train to work in the tall skyscrapers.

Cariños, Anna ♡

★ Grand Central Station has restaurants and stores.

★ The ceiling was painted as a sky with constellations.

★ The famous four-sided brass clock stands in the middle of the terminal.

Grand Central Station

★ La estación *Grand Central* tiene restaurantes y tiendas.

★ En el techo están pintados el cielo y las constelaciones.

★ El famoso reloj de metal de cuatro caras está en medio de la terminal.

5

6

Hi Madilynn,

Mom was happy tonight! We got dressed up and saw a Broadway play. It was amazing! Broadway is a street in Manhattan where some of the richest people live. Mom looked for movie stars, but she didn't see any.

See you later, Anna ♡

★ Only 4 theaters are actually on Broadway.

★ Broadway is called The Great White Way because of the lights.

★ Theater workshops are available for children who want to be in plays.

★ En Broadway realmente sólo hay cuatro teatros.

★ A Broadway se le llama La Gran Vía Blanca a causa de las luces.

★ Hay talleres de teatro para los niños que quieran participar en obras teatrales.

Dear Jackson,

Times Square is a busy intersection and neighborhood. New Yorkers celebrate here with a huge Thanksgiving Day parade. Giant helium balloons of cartoon characters float between the huge buildings. I can't wait to watch it on TV!

Take Care, Anna ♡

★ Over 200,000 people come through Times Square each day.

★ Many TV shows and movies have been filmed here.

★ New Year's Eve is celebrated by dropping a 200-pound ball at midnight.

Times Square

⭐ Más de 200,000 personas pasan por *Times Square* todos los días.

⭐ Aquí se han filmado muchas películas y series de televisión.

⭐ La víspera de Año Nuevo se celebra haciendo bajar una bola de 200 libras a medianoche desde lo alto de un edificio.

New York
Stock Exchange

Hola Margarita y José,

Dad went to the New York Stock Exchange on Wall Street today. He said hundreds of people were yelling and waving their arms when trading stocks. Businesses and banks throughout the world are affected by what happens here. Dad said it would be too stressful to work at the Stock Exchange.

Adiós, Anna ♡

★ Stocks and bonds are sold here.

★ The stock market crashed on Black Thursday, October 29, 1929.

★ This was the beginning of the Great Depression.

★ Aquí se venden bonos y acciones.

★ El mercado de valores sufrió una caída el llamado Jueves Negro, el 29 de octubre de 1929.

★ Éste fue el comienzo de la Gran Depresión.

Dearest Maureen and George,

Today we visited the Empire State Building. It was once the tallest building in the world. Every year there's a race to see who can run up 86 flights of steps the fastest. Someday I'm going to come back and win!

Love, Anna ♡

⭐ The Empire State Building stands more than a quarter mile into the sky.

⭐ There are observation decks on the 86th and 102nd floor.

⭐ The skyscraper sways slightly on windy days.

⭐ El edificio *Empire State* se eleva hacia el cielo más de una milla.

⭐ Hay miradores en los pisos 86 y 102.

⭐ El rascacielos se mece ligeramente en días ventosos.

Empire
State Building

13

World Trade Center Memorial

★ Almost 3,000 people died on September 11.

★ The Twin Towers each had 110 floors.

★ They are rebuilding on the site.

Saludos Juan,

Today we were sad when we visited the world Trade Center Memorial. The Twin Towers were destroyed on September 11, 2001 by terrorists. A memorial marks the spot now called Ground Zero. People leave flowers and notes to family and friends that they lost in this tragedy. I'll never forget this day.

Hasta luego, Anna ♡

★ Casi 3,000 personas murieron el 11 de septiembre.

★ Cada una de las Torres Gemelas tenía 110 pisos.

★ Se está reconstruyendo en el lugar.

Dear Kristina,

Today we walked across the mile long Brooklyn Bridge. Wow, what a hike! It took 14 years to build the suspension bridge. The main engineer died before the bridge was finished, so his son took over. When he was injured, he supervised from his bedroom. His wife took messages to the workers.

Take care, Anna ♡

⭐ The Brooklyn Bridge was the first to use steel and explosives while underwater.

⭐ Between 20-30 people were killed during the building of the bridge.

⭐ Over 100,000 vehicles and about 1,000 bikers go across the bridge each day.

Brooklyn Bridge

★ El puente de Brooklyn fue el primero en usar acero y explosivos bajo el agua para su construcción.

★ De 20 a 30 personas murieron durante la construcción del puente.

★ Más de 100,000 vehículos y cerca de 1,000 ciclistas cruzan el puente todos los días.

The Statue of Liberty

Dear Cindy and Ally,

The Statue of Liberty is the coolest! The 305-foot copper statue was a gift from France. Some say the sculptor, Frederic Bartoldi, made the face look like his mother. The frame was built in France, taken apart, and shipped to the United States on a boat. Workers put it back together in New York. Imagine that!

Miss you, Anna ♡

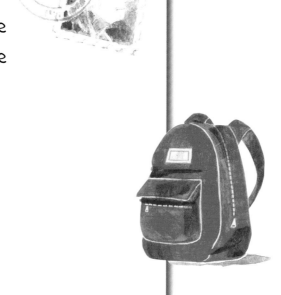

★ The 7 spikes on her crown represent the 7 continents.

★ Gustave Eiffel engineered this statue and the Eiffel Tower in París.

★ There are stairs and an elevator, but you cannot go to the top.

★ Las 7 puntas de su corona representan los 7 continentes.

★ Gustave Eiffel, el creador de la torre Eiffel de París, diseñó esta estatua.

★ Tiene escaleras y un elevador en su interior, pero no está permitido subir hasta arriba.

Buenos días, Amelia,

Today we visited the Ellis Island Immigration Museum. Between 1892 and 1954, almost 12 million people came here from other countries. Doctors checked each person to make sure they didn't bring any diseases into the United States.

Sinceramente, Anna ♡

★ The American Immigration Wall of Honor has over 400,000 names on it.

★ Over 40% of Americans today have ancestors that came through Ellis Island.

★ Most of the immigrants came from Ireland, Poland, Germany and Russia.

Ellis Island Immigration Museum

★ En la sala que honra a los inmigrantes de los Estados Unidos hay una pared donde aparecen más de 400,000 nombres.

★ Más del 40% de los estadounidenses tienen ancestros que llegaron por Ellis Island.

★ La mayoría de los inmigrantes vinieron de Irlanda, Polonia, Alemania y Rusia.

Central Park

⭐ A carousel plays music as children ride it.

⭐ People enjoy remote control boats on the boat pond.

⭐ Central Park is home to one of the oldest public zoos.

Dear Aunt Jackie and Uncle Larry,

I love Central Park. The park is over 2 miles long and was built on a swamp! After a picnic, we walked in the gardens and woodlands and canoed in the lake. Mom said if we visited in the winter, we could go ice-skating in here too. That would be so much fun!

Love you, Anna ♡

★ Un carrusel toca música mientras da vueltas.

★ La gente disfruta los botes de control remoto en el estanque.

★ El parque Central tiene uno de los zoológicos públicos más antiguos.

Dear Mark and Michelle,

Today we went to a New York Knicks basketball game at Madison Square Garden. Over 19,000 people cheered in the stands. Did you know the Knicks played the first NBA game ever? I want to come back for basketball camp!

Take care, Anna ♡

★ It is nicknamed The Garden or MSG.

★ The New York Rangers hockey team also plays here.

★ Some call it The Most Famous Arena.

Madison Square Garden

⭐ Lo llaman *The Garden* o MSG.

⭐ Aquí también juegan los *Rangers*, el equipo de hockey de Nueva York.

⭐ Hay quienes lo llaman el estadio más famoso.

Dear Terri and Lisa,

We toured the United Nations headquarters today. The 192 countries of the UN work together to make the world a better place. The UN was started after World War II to try to prevent another big war. We saw a meeting of the Security Council. I wonder what they were talking about.

Sincerely, Anna ♡

★ In 2000, about 150 world leaders met here to discuss world issues.
★ The UN also helps poor people, the environment and endangered animals.
★ Tours are given in over 30 languages including Spanish, French, Portuguese, and Arabic.

★ En el año 2000, 150 líderes mundiales se reunieron aquí para discutir asuntos mundiales.
★ La ONU también ayuda a los países pobres, al medio ambiente y a los animales en peligro de extinción.
★ Se ofrecen giras en más de 30 idiomas incluyendo español, francés, portugués y árabe.

27

Carlos,

Today we went to Chinatown. Dad made us try some Chinese dumplings called dim sum. They were delicious! I had a hard time with those chopsticks though. We also saw the parade for the Chinese New Year. This year is the year of the rat. Isn't that funny? Happy Chinese New Year!

Nos vemos pronto, Anna

★ People wear red to the New Year's Celebration.

★ The dragon in the parade can be over 100 feet long.

★ The dragon is believed to bring good luck.

★ La gente se viste de rojo en la celebración del Año Nuevo.

★ El dragón en el desfile puede medir más de 100 pies.

★ Se cree que el dragón atrae la buena suerte.

New Year's Celebration
in Chinatown

29

Yankee Stadium

★ Yankee Stadium is called The House That Ruth Built.

★ Babe Ruth hit 714 home runs in his career.

★ The New York Yankees have won more World Series titles than any other team.

Dear Uncle Phil,

Today was exciting because I learned all about the old Yankee Stadium. Dad told me that in 1923 Grandpa went to the first game ever played here. He was in the stands when Babe Ruth hit a home run! It was the first home run in this stadium. Babe Ruth was one of the best players ever.

See you soon, Anna ♡

⭐ Al estadio de los Yankees se le conoce como la casa que Ruth construyó.

⭐ Babe Ruth bateó 714 jonrones durante su carrera.

⭐ Los Yankees de Nueva York han ganado más series mundiales que cualquier otro equipo.

So, that was my trip to New York City! I learned so much about The Big Apple. I can't wait to go back!

Bueno, ¡ése fue mi viaje a Nueva York! Aprendí mucho sobre La Gran Manzana. ¡Estoy impaciente por volver!